Joey Daring Caring and Curious

For my daughters, with love.—MMC

For my 2 m's, I love you no matter what.—JLV

Published by
MAGINATION PRESS
An Educational Publishing Foundation Book
American Psychological Association
750 First Street, NE
Washington, DC 20002

For more information about our books, including a complete catalog, please write to us, call 1-800-374-2721, or visit our website at www.apa.org/pubs/magination.

Book design by Susan K. White
Printed by Phoenix Color Corporation, Hagerstown, MD

Library of Congress Cataloging-in-Publication Data
Craver, Marcella Marino.
Joey daring, caring, and curious : how a mischief maker uncovers unconditional love / by Marcella Marino Craver, MSEd, CAS ; illustrated by Joanne Lew-Vriethoff.
pages cm
"American Psychological Association."
Summary: Mom reassures Joey that she loves her children equally, even mischievous Joey.
ISBN-13: 978-1-4338-1652-9 (hardcover)
ISBN-10: 1-4338-1652-0 (hardcover)
ISBN-13: 978-1-4338-1653-6 (pbk.)
ISBN-10: 1-4338-1653-9 (pbk.)
[1. Love—Fiction. 2. Mother and child—Fiction. 3. Behavior—Fiction.] I. Lew-Vriethoff, Joanne, illustrator. II. Title.
PZ7.C8537Jo 2014
[E]—dc23   2013048298

Manufactured in the United States of America

10 9 8 7 6 5 4 3 2 1

Joey Daring Caring and Curious

How a Mischief Maker
Uncovers Unconditional LOVE

by Marcella Marino Craver, MSEd, CAS

illustrated by
Joanne Lew-Vriethoff

MAGINATION PRESS • WASHINGTON, DC
American Psychological Association

Joey kept thinking the same unpleasant thing over and over.
He thought of it at night. He thought of it in school.
He even thought of it while eating ice cream at the park!

Finally, he thought: just ask Mom!
But could he? Could he ask her that question?
If he asked Mom, what would she say?
The more he thought about it, the more he felt like he knew
what she would say and he wouldn't like to hear it.

Joey sawed with his stick and thought hard.

Joey tried to ask Mom before school but...

He tried to ask her outside but...

He tried to ask her
after dinner but...

Joey, now more worried than before,
bravely wrote Mom a note.

He held his breath as he
slipped it under her pillow.

When Joey found the note, he did not understand.
Three checks! He was sure Mom liked Jake and Olivia more.
Jake was bigger, faster, and helpful. Olivia was little, sweet, and
Mom loved to dress her in pink—something Joey would never
wear! Joey knew he acted daring and curious sometimes,
but he was caring too. Now he had more questions.
Could he ask the one that gave him the chills?

He tried to ask Mom on Saturday but...

He tried to ask her on Sunday but...

He tried to ask her
one more time but...

He could write the question,
but did he really want to know
the answer? It could be terrible news,
but he just needed to know! He bit his lip
and wrote a second note.

All day long, he tried not to think of the note.

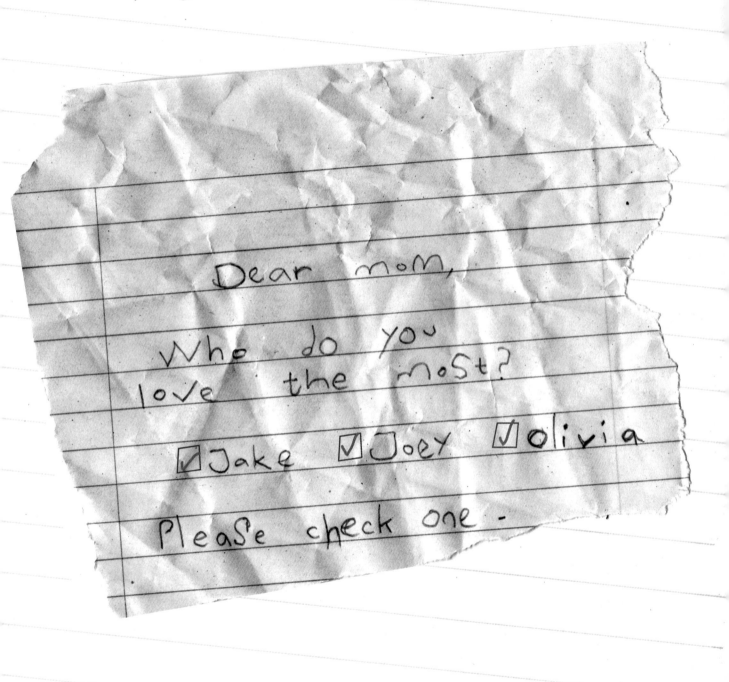

How could this be? He made the most mischief in the house, and Olivia and Jake were perfect!

How could Mom check all of the boxes on both notes?

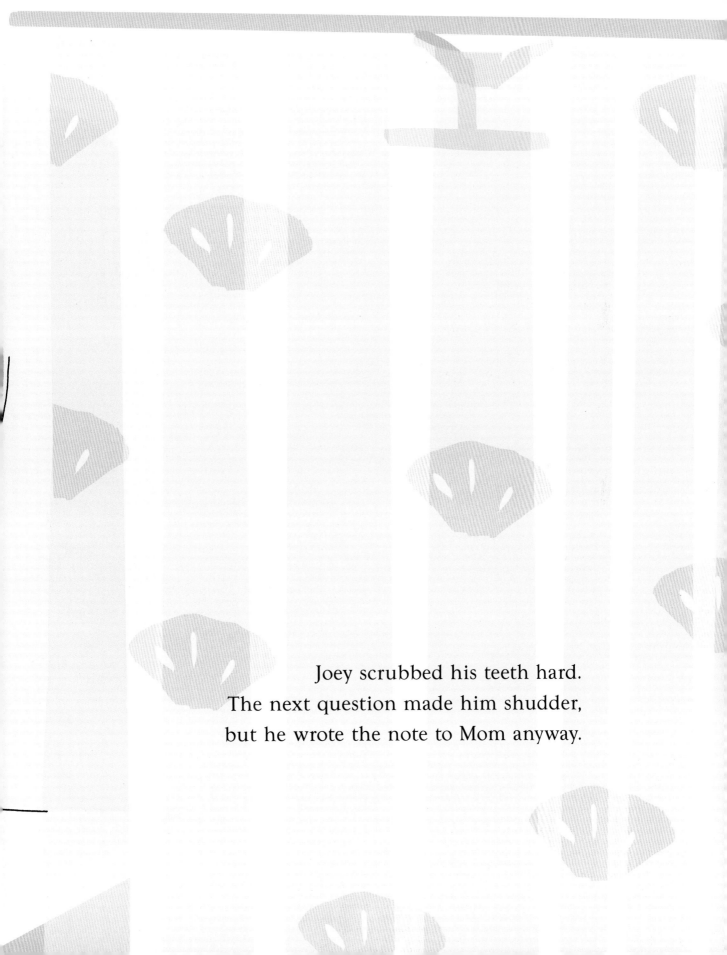

Joey scrubbed his teeth hard.
The next question made him shudder,
but he wrote the note to Mom anyway.

Joey hid under his blanket
with the lights on to wait
for the news.

Mom gently removed the
covers from Joey's head
and hugged him tight
for a long time.

Joey peeked and saw.

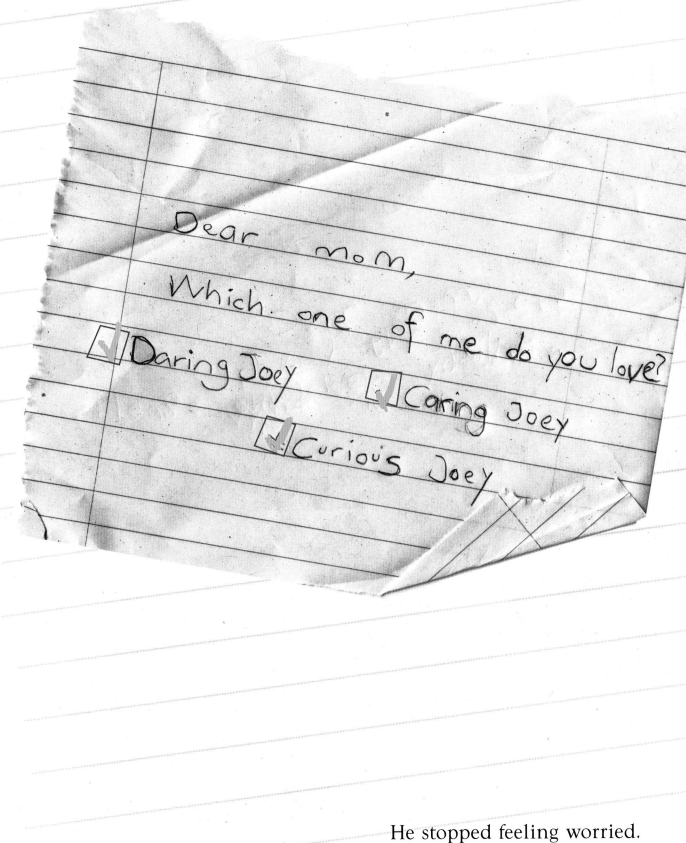

He stopped feeling worried.
Mom said what he knew in his heart all along.

"I'll love you, Jake, and Olivia forever with all my heart.
Even if you are making mischief or don't feel loveable,
even when you are acting daring, caring, or curious,
I love you. No matter what."

Note to Parents & Other Caregivers

by Elizabeth McCallum, PhD

The childhood years are filled with breaking rules and testing limits. As parents, we have all experienced the embarrassment or frustration of an unruly or misbehaving child. While, at times, we may want to throw up our hands in defeat, it is important to recognize that some defiance is a normal part of child development and can actually be a learning tool in a child's developing understanding of predicting consequences for behaviors. Childhood defiance can be a natural experiment through which children learn those behaviors that lead to desired consequences (praise, smiles, rewards, etc.), and those behaviors that lead to less desired consequences (time-out, redirection, etc.).

Particularly as children gain independence from their parents and develop a sense of self, their behavior may deviate from those behaviors preferred by parents—sometimes significantly! Children are testing the boundaries of acceptable behaviors and learning valuable lessons about cause and effect in the meantime.

How This Book Can Help
Joey Daring Caring and Curious is a delightful story about a young boy named Joey who has concerns that his mother may prefer his siblings over himself. Joey is more rambunctious and mischievous than his studious older brother Jake and his sweet baby sister Olivia. Through the actions of the story, Joey comes to learn that his mother loves each of them for who they are, unconditionally, mischief and all.

This book can serve as a great tool for discussing parents' unconditional love for their child. Parents may want to emphasize that, although they may not always love the ways their child behaves, they will always love their child for who he or she is as an individual. After reading the book, you may wish to ask your child if he notices any of Joey's behaviors or feelings that he may also be experiencing. This may help you to identify and address specific stressors in your child's life.

Encouraging Appropriate Behavior
Although parents cannot eliminate all frustrating or annoying child behaviors, there are ways to decrease their frequency and increase positive parent-child interactions.

- **Spend quality time with each of your children daily.** Try to make time to spend alone with each of your children each day, even if it revolves around simple tasks such as cooking or cleaning together. For school-aged children, you might spend a little time discussing their school day or assisting with homework assignments. This individual time conveys the message that each child is deserving of your undivided attention.

- **Encourage your child to discuss concerns and feelings.** Try to acknowledge your child's feelings of stress and discuss the events in his life that may be causing it. Let your child know that it is safe to share his feelings with you and that doing so will allow you to better help him find coping strategies. When your child does wish to share feelings, listen to him without evaluating the rationality or irrationality of those feelings.

- **Find and emphasize your child's strengths.** Every child has strengths. Perhaps your child is kind and makes friends easily; she may excel at athletics; or your child may be adept at academic tasks. Whatever the domain, emphasizing your child's unique talents will help build self-confidence and provide him or her with a context for thinking about putting these skills to good use.

- **Set realistic expectations for behavior.** In the story, Joey is concerned that his mother prefers his siblings over him because he tends to make more mischief. It is important to match your expectations for your child's behavior to his age and developmental level. Remember that all children are different and what may have come easily to your older child may be more difficult for your younger one.

When minor behavioral problems arise, the best method may be to simply ignore the behaviors and redirect the child to alternate activities or topics.

Remember that you are the best resource for encouraging your child to behave appropriately. One way to do this is to reassure your child that you love him unconditionally, even when you don't love his actions. However, if you believe that your child's defiance goes beyond that of normal childhood behavior or if your child exhibits behaviors that could be dangerous to himself or others, you should discuss your concerns with his school psychologist, school counselor, or a licensed psychologist.

Elizabeth McCallum, PhD, is an associate professor in the School Psychology program at Duquesne University, as well as a Pennsylvania certified school psychologist. She is the author of many scholarly journal articles and book chapters on topics including academic and behavioral interventions for children and adolescents.

About the Author

Marcella Marino Craver, MSEd, CAS, recently started a new career as a school counselor after nineteen years as a school psychologist in New Jersey and New York public schools. She is the author of *Learn to Study: A Comprehensive Guide to Academic Success* and *Chillax! How Ernie Learns to Chill Out, Relax, and Take Charge of His Anger. Chillax!* was awarded the Mom's Choice Gold Award for Juvenile Books—Self-Improvement and the Gold Moonbeam Children's Book Award for Comic Books/Graphic Novels. Her most recent book, *Shield Up! How Upstanding Bystanders Stop Bullying*, was released in August 2014. Marcella lives with her wonderful husband, their two musically inclined teenagers, and a playful cat, who all fill her life with love, music, and laughter.

About the Illustrator

Joanne Lew-Vriethoff is a talented artist whose passion for stories is shown through her amazing, whimsical illustrations in picture and chapter books. Joanne is married with two lovely children, a girl and a boy. Together, they discover the world by traveling and deriving inspiration for her art. Joanne also enjoys photographing street art and supporting women as a trained doula. A veritable global citizen, she currently lives in Asia where she is re-connecting with her roots and continuing the adventure.

About Magination Press

Magination Press publishes self-help books for kids and the adults in their lives. Magination Press is an imprint of the American Psychological Association, the largest scientific and professional organization representing psychologists in the United States and the largest association of psychologists worldwide.